This is Otto.

Otto is a penguin chick
who has a very important
job to do . . .

The Penguin Who Wanted to Find Out

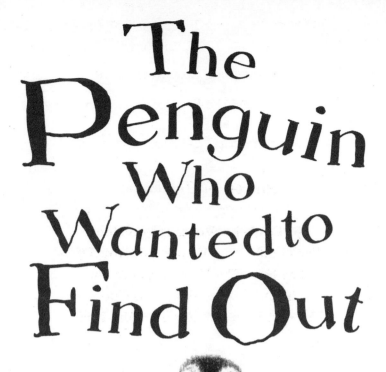

JILL TOMLINSON

Pictures by Paul Howard

Originally published as *Penguin's Progress*

EGMONT

For David, who has been to the Antarctic,

his wife, Pat, and the boys, James, Peter and

Matthew, and of course Claudius

The Penguin Who Wanted to Find Out
First published in Great Britain 1975
by Methuen Children's Books Ltd as *Penguin's Progress*

First published in this edition 2004 by Egmont Books Limited
This edition published 2013 by Dean,
an imprint of Egmont UK Limited
The Yellow Building, 1 Nicholas Road, London W11 4AN

Text copyright © 1975 The Estate of Jill Tomlinson
Cover and illustrations copyright © 2004 Paul Howard

The moral rights of the author and illustrator have been asserted

ISBN 978 0 6035 6922 7

56906/1

A CIP catalogue record for this title is available from the British Library

Printed and bound in Great Britain by the CPI Group

MIX
Paper
FSC   FSC® C018306

Egmont is passionate about helping to preserve the world's remaining ancient forests.
We only use paper from legal and sustainable forest sources, so we know where every
single tree comes from that goes into every paper that makes up every book.

This book is made from paper certified by the Forestry Stewardship Council (FSC),
an organisation dedicated to promoting responsible management of forest resources.
For more information on the FSC, please visit **www.fsc.org**. To learn more about
Egmont's sustainable paper policy, please visit **www.egmont.co.uk/ethical**.

Contents

 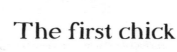

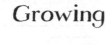 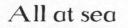

It is cold

Otto was a penguin chick. He lived on his
father's feet at the bottom of the world.
That's what Leo said, anyway, that they
lived at the bottom of the world. Leo was
another penguin chick and he lived on *his*
father's feet. That is how Otto met him.

Their fathers Claudius and Nero were friends and when they stopped to talk to each other, beak to beak, Otto and Leo were almost beak to beak too. They had to shout a bit because Claudius and Nero were rather fat, like all the other penguins, so their tummies kept Otto and Leo rather far apart.

'How do you know we're at the bottom of the world?' Otto yelled across to Leo one morning.

'Your father told my father,' said Leo. 'Your father knows everything.'

'What?' yelled Otto.

'Your father knows everything,' Leo squealed back. 'Everyone goes to Claudius when they want to know anything.'

'I know that,' Otto complained bitterly. 'I can never get a word in!'

'What are you two bellowing about down there?' said a deep voice above their heads.

'Oh, Dad, there are so many things I want to know about and you never even talk to me,' Otto shouted, looking up.

A beak came down and Otto looked into Claudius's face for the first time.

'I hadn't realized how grown up you are now, Otto. I'm not your father, by the way. Call me Claudius, not Dad.'

'Why aren't you my father?'

'Because I found you in the snow when you were an egg and decided to look after you and keep you warm until you could look after yourself.'

'Didn't my own father want me then?'

'Oh, it wasn't that at all. You probably rolled off his feet when he wasn't looking. Very rolly things, eggs are. Anyway, you're all right now. You've got me.'

Otto was worried. 'But I might have fallen off,' he said.

'Fallen off what?'

'The world. Leo said this is the bottom of the world.'

'Well, it is. Antarctica it's called, the South Pole. But you won't fall off.'

'Why not?'

'Because I say so. What else do you want to ask me?'

'What am I?'

'A penguin. An emperor penguin.'

'I know that. I mean what is a penguin?'

'A bird. Now we'll have to stop talking and join the huddle of penguins, because the wind is getting up and it will be very cold soon.'

'Soon!' squeaked Otto. 'It's cold all the time!'

'It will feel even colder if you don't join the other penguins. Come on.'

Claudius began to shuffle across the ice towards the other penguins who were already huddling together to keep warm.

'Aren't there a lot of us?' Otto yelled up to Claudius.

'That's good,' Claudius boomed back at

the chick on his feet. 'The more there are, the warmer we'll be. Now keep your beak shut and snuggle as close as you can to me. There's a real blizzard coming.'

Otto did what he was told but it was very difficult to keep his beak shut. He wanted to

know what a blizzard was.

He soon found out. The wind got stronger and stronger and it felt colder and colder. Snow was driven at them harder and harder. They pressed closer and closer together to keep warm.

Soon they were too close. Otto had to open his beak: 'Claudius! Claudius! I'm getting squashed.'

He couldn't see Claudius's head because the snow blotted it out, but a voice came back through the howl of the wind.

'It's all right, Otto, get under that feathery flap below my tummy. That will protect you. Now, keep your beak shut until I say you can open it.'

Otto squeezed as hard as he could under Claudius's tummy away from the back of the penguin in front and those pressing in from each side. He had never been so cold. He thought that the snow and the wind would go on for ever. But they didn't: the wind died down and the penguins began to move apart. When he had room to bend his head

Claudius called down to Otto: 'Otto, Otto, are you all right?'

Otto stirred and he said feebly, 'Mmm, mmm, mmmm.'

Claudius was worried. 'What's the matter with you? Speak up!'

'MMM, MMM, MMM,' Otto squeaked as loudly as he could.

Claudius was puzzled. He bent down and looked closely at Otto.

'Are you all right?'

'MMMMM.'

Claudius began to laugh.

'I see. It's all my fault. You can open your beak now.'

'Oh, thank goodness,' said Otto, gasping with relief. 'It's very difficult talking with your beak shut.'

'It must be,' Claudius said. 'Anyway, did you keep warm?'

'No, I didn't. I'm cold. I don't like being cold.'

'I don't expect you to like it. You'll just have to get used to it, because we live in a cold place.'

'Can't we live somewhere else?'

'No.'

Claudius wasn't worried about Otto any more. People only complain when they are feeling better.

'I don't think I'll ever get used to being so cold,' said Otto.

'You will. I'll help you keep warm while you're little, and when you grow up you'll be covered in blubber like me. That helps a lot.'

Otto looked up at Claudius.

'Will I really be as fat as you?'

'Yes, all grown-up penguins are fat.'

'Coo,' said Otto. 'Oh well, I suppose I'll get used to it.'

The first chick

'What are you doing?' Claudius complained one morning. 'If you bounce on my feet any more you'll plant me in the snow and I'll never move again. And stop waving your flippers about like that. It feels like a blizzard blowing up there.'

Otto didn't stop. 'I'm trying to fly,' he shouted. 'You said I'm a bird. Birds fly, don't they?'

'Penguins don't fly,' Claudius said. 'Now stop jumping on my feet and I'll tell you what penguins do.'

Otto stopped. He was getting tired anyway. 'What do penguins do?' he asked, a little breathlessly.

'They swim. That's like flying in the sea. They're very good at it too.'

Otto looked up at Claudius.

'I want to fly up high like that bird up there. It's going round and round in the sky, and I want to do that.'

'Well you can't, so don't start bouncing again. Anyway, what bird?' Claudius was looking up. 'Oh my goodness, a skua. Now stay close to me, Otto. Nasty things, skuas. They like chicks.'

Otto was puzzled. 'Are you nasty then,

Claudius?'

'Am I . . .? Oh, I see! I like chicks, but not for dinner. A skua will dive down from the sky and steal a nice juicy penguin chick for its next meal. That's why you mustn't wander off by yourself.'

'I didn't know I could wander off by myself,' Otto said. 'I'm stuck on your feet.'

'Not for ever, thank goodness,' Claudius said, shifting his poor trampled toes. 'You're nearly big enough to walk beside me now, and soon you'll have all the other chicks to play with.'

'What other chicks?' Otto said. 'There's only Leo and me.'

'There are lots of other chicks now, you'll find. You and Leo were the first chicks to hatch, but you aren't the only ones. When that skua has gone I'll take you round and you'll see what a lot of you there are.'

Claudius was right. All the grown-ups seemed to be shuffling around with chicks on their feet. Every round white tummy had a little head peeping out under it. Nearly every round white tummy, that is, because Otto was waddling along beside Claudius. Leo couldn't believe his eyes when he saw Otto coming towards him.

'Otto!' He shouted up at Nero. 'Dad, look! Otto's walking by himself.'

'Oh yes,' said Nero. 'You can go and meet him if you like.'

'Me?' Leo said. 'By myself?'

'Yes, go on. You're big enough now.'

Leo looked at the ice all around him. He wasn't at all sure that he wanted to leave the shelter of Nero's nice warm feet.

'Won't my feet get cold?'

'Not very,' said a voice quite near him.
It was Otto. 'Come on, Leo. We're the first
chicks. That's very special. We have to show
all the little ones what to do.'

'I don't *know* what to do,' said Leo.
'Anyway, you may be the first chick but I'm
only the second. I'm not at all sure that I'm
ready yet.'

Nero was
sure. He tipped
Leo on to the ice
and walked across
to talk to Claudius.
Leo squeaked, picked
himself up and ran after Nero, but Otto
headed him off.

'Catch me!' he called, running a little way. 'I bet you can't.'

Leo couldn't resist hat, so a chase began. It lasted a long time. Claudius and Nero watched the two downy little chicks tumbling about in the snow having a wonderful time.

'Let's join them,' Claudius said suddenly.

'Join them?' Nero said. 'I'm too old for that sort of fun and games.'

'No, you're not,' Claudius said. 'It's going to be the easiest way to collect them up. Come on, I bet you can't catch me.'

So then there were four of them in the game and they had a lot of fun. One of the new chicks wanted to join in but his father wouldn't let him.

'No, not yet. When you're a bit older you can.'

The new chick was very disappointed, but a little later Claudius and Nero went past with Otto and Leo back on their feet. Otto saw the new little chick watching and called out, 'Hello. What's your name?'

'Gusto. Can I play with you next time?'

'You can play with us when your dad says you can. You're not big enough yet.'

'I'm not very big outside, but I'm *enormous* inside,' Gusto said.

Claudius laughed above Otto's head as they moved on.

'You're going to have trouble with that one, Otto,' he said.

'I am?' Otto said. 'He has a father, hasn't he? I won't have to look after him.'

'You will,' Claudius said. 'You're the first chick so you'll have to look after the whole clutch.'

'You mean all of them?'

Otto looked around slowly. There were penguins as far as he could see and nearly all of them had chicks or eggs on their feet.

'No, just your own gang around here. They'll keep you busy, though.'

They did. A few days later Otto and Leo had lots of new friends. When it was warm enough they tumbled from their fathers' feet and played together. The very little ones like Gusto just didn't understand that they must stay together to be safe. Otto, watching the skuas circling hopefully above them, had to keep rounding them up.

'Gusto!' he was always having to yell.

'Come back, you must stay close to me.'

'Why?' said Gusto. 'I only want to see what's over there.'

'Because I say so. You'll end up as a skua's dinner if you wander round by yourself. We must all stay together to be safe. Come on.'

'Oh, all right,' Gusto said, wandering back into the group. 'But I can look after myself. You are *bossy*, Otto.'

Nero and all the other fathers were very glad that Otto was bossy. They didn't have to worry about their chicks very much.

'Your Otto looks after them all beautifully,' one said to Claudius. 'You must be very proud, Claudius.'

Claudius *was* very proud. Otto didn't know it, though. He came back to Claudius one night and called up to him.

'Claudius, am I bossy?'

'Yes,' said Claudius. 'Very.'

'Oh dear,' Otto said. 'They keep telling me I am, but how else can I keep them safe?'

'How else?' Claudius said. 'You be bossy. First chicks always have to be bossy. You'll soon learn that.'

Penguins look after each other

Claudius blinked the sleep from his eyes
and pointed his beak towards the voice at
his feet.

'Yes, Otto, what is it?'

'I have a very funny feeling in my tummy.
An asking sort of feeling. What is it?'

'You're hungry, I expect.'

'What's hungry?'

'An asking feeling in your tummy. I've got it too. We need something to eat. We'll have to go and see if the ladies are back from the sea.'

'The ladies?'

'Yes, they've been eating fish and things in the sea so that they can feed you chicks. I'll find you a nice aunty and she'll feed you with shrimp soup. It's delicious. You'll like that, and that empty feeling will go away for a bit.'

'Will you have some too, Claudius?'

'Well, no. I shall have to say goodbye to you and go off to the sea to find lots of food. I've had nothing to eat all winter and I'm very hungry.'

'You mean you'll go away without me?'

'Yes, Otto. You're not big enough to come

to the sea yet.'

Otto was horrified. 'You wouldn't leave me, Claudius. I need you.'

'No you don't. I'll find a nice aunty to look after you. She'll be just as good as me, and you'll still have me inside. That's the important place to have a good dad – inside.'

'But I want you *outside* where I can see you. Oh, don't leave me, Claudius.'

Poor Otto was shattered. But Claudius began to lead him towards the sea and the journey was so interesting that Otto began to forget how miserable he was. He had never been away from the rookery of penguins before. The white ice stretched round them as far as he could see.

'The bottom of the world is very big,' he said at last.

'Yes, Antarctica is very big,' Claudius said. 'Look, over there. A Weddell seal and her pup.'

Otto looked. A huge fat creature lay on the ice with a smaller one cuddled up to her.

'Marvellous divers, seals are,' Claudius said. 'They can dive much deeper than us.'

'Dive?' Otto asked.

'Go a very long way down into the water,' explained Claudius. 'You'll see them go past you when *you're* in the sea.'

'What do they do when there's a blizzard?' Otto said. 'There don't seem to be any others around to huddle with.'

'No, they just have to hope they're fat enough to keep warm. They're almost solid blubber so they're usually all right.'

'The chick . . . the pup, I mean, has a

nice face,' Otto said, as they got nearer to the seals. 'What are those hairy bits on his face?'

'Whiskers,' Claudius said. 'All seals have whiskers. Now look carefully at those seals because they're Weddell seals and they look a bit like leopard seals. You must learn never to get them mixed up.'

'Why?' asked Otto. 'Aren't leopard seals nice?'

'No, not nice at all. They eat penguins. Weddell seals only eat fish and things and they're quite harmless. But you must watch out for leopard seals when you first go to sea. Weddells have smaller heads and in time you will learn the difference, but at first it's best to keep away from all spotted seals.'

Otto suddenly stopped dead.

'Claudius, the ice is moving!' he shouted.

'Look at it!'

'That's the sea,' Claudius said. 'And look, there's someone coming to meet us. One of the ladies, I expect.'

It was. She kept shaking herself to get rid of the water on her feathers before it turned to ice. As she came nearer to them Claudius suddenly said, 'It's Anna. She'll make a good aunty for you.'

Otto moved and hid himself behind Claudius's back.

'I don't want an aunty. I want to keep my dad.'

Claudius turned round and rubbed the top of Otto's head with his beak.

'Sorry, Otto,' he said. 'But you are an emperor penguin and emperor penguins have to get used to lots of different mothers and fathers when they are growing up.'

Otto looked up at Claudius. 'But the seal pup had someone all to himself. I want you all to myself.'

'Of course you do, but you have a nice huddle of friends to belong to. That seal pup hasn't got anything like that. Penguins look after each other. Will you look after me?'

Otto gaped at him.

'How? You're going away.'

'Will you let me go and feed myself? I'm starving. My asking feeling inside really hurts. You can help me by letting me go.'

Otto didn't know what to say. But he knew what he had to do. He waddled round to the front of Claudius again and looked towards Anna. 'She's not bad, I suppose,' he agreed at last.

Claudius tapped Otto's head with his beak.

'Thank you,' he said. Then he called out, 'Anna, I have a hungry chick here waiting for you.'

Anna began to waddle even faster towards them.

'Open your beak, Otto,' Claudius said.

'I don't feel like talking.'

'Not to talk. So that Anna can feed you,' laughed Claudius. 'Anna, this is Otto. He's our first chick this year.'

'Oh, I shall be very proud to be *his* aunty then. Hello, Otto. You must be very hungry. Open your beak and I'll give you some fish soup.'

It was good. In a few minutes the empty feeling in Otto's tummy had nearly gone. Anna moved back, taking her beak out of Otto's.

'More,' Otto said. 'Please, Anna.'

'Come on then,' Anna said. 'I'm glad you like what I've brought you.'

So Otto had his first meal.

Claudius went down to the sea to have *his* first meal of the winter when he saw that Otto was all right. He knew that Anna would look after him well.

When Otto was quite full he stood back from his new aunty and saw that Claudius had gone. The ice stretched around them white and empty. Otto's head drooped. No more Claudius. How could he live without Claudius? Anna understood.

'Come on, Otto,' she said. 'Claudius will soon be full too. Will you show me the way home?'

Otto turned round slowly and began to lead the way. What had Claudius said to him? Penguins help each other. And he was a penguin. He would have to get used to it!

The last chick

Otto was so busy during the next few days that
he didn't have much time to miss Claudius.
As the ladies came back from the sea to feed
the chicks all the fathers disappeared one by
one to feed themselves. Otto had to look after
all his huddle. Often he had to huddle the
chicks together when the grown-ups were still
walking about. They had enough blubber to
keep them warm but the chicks hadn't yet.

When they began to feel the cold Otto and Leo collected all the chicks together in a tight huddle, the little ones in the centre where it was warmest. When he had finished making the very first chick huddle of this kind, Otto noticed a chick standing all by himself some way away, looking out to sea.

'Oh dear,' he said to Leo. 'Look, we've left someone out. I must go and fetch him.'

Leo looked across at the chick.

'Oh yes, that's Alex. He was the last chick to hatch so he's only a baby. We must keep him warm.'

Otto hurried off. As he got nearer to the chick he could see that Leo was right. Alex was just a baby. He wasn't really big enough to be off his father's feet. He looked so cold and miserable standing there that Otto knew he must get him into the huddle quickly.

'Where's Daddy?' wailed Alex, as soon
as Otto reached him. 'I want my father.'

'I expect he was hungry,' Otto said.
'Aren't you hungry?'

'That's what that lady penguin asked
me,' Alex said. 'I didn't know what she
meant, so she went away. What's hungry?'

Otto looked at him. 'It's an asking feeling
inside, but I don't expect you have it yet. So
you haven't got an aunty?'

'No, I haven't got anybody at all.'

Otto felt very fatherly. 'My name is
Otto,' he said. 'You stay close to me and
I'll look after you. Come on, we must get
back to our huddle.'

Alex waddled along beside Otto for a few
yards and then he stopped.

'Otto!' he wailed. Otto stopped too.

'What's the matter?'

'You're not a proper father at all,' Alex said. 'Your feet aren't big enough.'

Otto looked down at his feet. Alex was quite right.

'No, I can't give you a ride yet,' he said. 'But perhaps my feet will grow in the warmth of the huddle, so let's hurry there. Come on, run.'

So Otto and Alex arrived at the huddle at last, Otto pushing the baby in front of him for the last little bit. He tried to push him to the centre of the huddle but Alex wouldn't leave him.

'I want to stay with you, Otto,' he said, standing firmly on Otto's feet. 'You can be my father now.'

Gusto was standing near them and he began to screech with laughter.

'Old bossy chick has a baby,' he shouted.

'When you're quite finished, cheeky chick, you can come and help me look after him,' Otto said. 'Come on. You keep his front warm while I keep the wind off his back.'

'Why?' said Gusto. 'I'm busy keeping myself warm.'

'Because penguins, emperor penguins anyway, look after each other. Come on, put your tummy against his. That's right. Alex, this is Gusto. He talks an awful lot, but he's a very nice chap.'

Alex looked shyly up at Gusto. 'If you talk a lot, you must be able to tell stories? I do like stories. Please tell me a story.'

Gusto looked helplessly at Otto.

'I've never told a story. Where do I get
it from?'

'Out of your head. I'm sure there are lots
in yours. Just begin "Once upon a time" and
carry on from there.'

So Gusto began. Soon Otto's worries
about little Alex were over. He was so happy
listening to Gusto's stories that he didn't even
notice how cold he was. Not until it got a bit
warmer and the huddle began to drift apart.
Gusto was hungry so he gabbled the end of
his last story and went off to find his aunty.

'Otto,' Alex wailed, 'Gusto's gone. I'm
cold, horribly cold.'

'Yes, Alex, I expect you are. We live in
a cold place you see. You'll get used to it.'

'Have you got used to it yet, Otto?'

'Well, no, not quite. I'm only a chick like you, you know. When we get bigger and fatter we won't feel so cold. The way to do that is to eat. Come on. I'm going to find aunty Anna.'

They found aunty Anna and Otto had a good feed. When he had finished he was very surprised to see Alex come up to Anna and say: 'Me, too.'

'What's this?' Otto said. 'I thought you weren't hungry yet?'

'I think I am now,' Alex said. 'Will you be my aunty, Anna?'

'Well, I don't know,' Anna said. '*Two* chicks to feed. I shall be worn out.'

Otto looked at her. 'Alex is the last chick around here, Anna. It means that you'll have the first and the last. That's very special.'

Anna grinned at Otto. 'All right, you've talked me into it. We'll find Alex an aunty of his own soon, but I'll feed him for the time being. Come on, little one.'

So Alex had his first meal. An enormous one.

'There won't be much left for you tomorrow, Otto,' Anna said. 'I'll have to go down to the sea again. Never mind. There'll be plenty of aunts and uncles coming to feed you all from now on.'

'You mean I'll have to get used to somebody different?' Otto asked. 'I've only just got to know you.'

'That's how it is with emperor penguins. The grown-ups go backwards and forwards to the sea to get food for you until you're big enough to go yourselves. You'll have lots of different penguins to look after you but you won't go hungry. Penguins look after each other.'

That's what Claudius said, Otto thought. But lots of different penguins to feed him! Oh well, he was a penguin. He'd get used to it.

Pup

Next day, when Otto was going down to the sea to try to find someone bringing up food, he saw something huge and fat lying on the ice: a seal. He was quite pleased at first, because it would be somebody to talk to. But as he got nearer Otto could see that the seal was spotted. What had Claudius said? 'Spotted seals might be leopard seals and they are dangerous.' This one didn't look very dangerous. He was so fat he could hardly move, and he was playing a sort of rolling game with himself. Then he saw Otto and waved a flipper. Otto thought he knew that face. He kept moving. Sure enough, it was the pup he had seen before with Claudius, but he was very much bigger now. Otto stopped a little distance away from the seal. The seal was so fat he could hardly move and even though Otto was no great mover he reckoned he could get out of the way if it were a leopard seal.

'Hello,' Otto said. 'Haven't I met you before?'

'You've passed me before. You didn't talk to me,' said the seal.

'I'm sorry,' Otto said. 'I was with Claudius and he was in a hurry. He was hungry.'

'That sounds like my mother,' said the seal. 'She's taught me to catch fish and look after myself. So now she's gone back to sea to feed herself again. She'd got terribly thin. Her bones were sticking out.'

'I can't say the same for you,' said Otto.

The seal laughed. 'No, I got fat very quickly, and as I got fatter my mother got thinner. It was all the milk I had, you see.'

'Milk?' said Otto. 'What's milk?'

'Well, it's what I was fed on,' said the seal. 'I'm a mammal, you see.'

'What's a mammal?' said Otto.

'Well, I expect you came out of an egg, didn't you, because you're a bird. Well, mammals don't. Seals are the only mammals in Antarctica. My mother told me that and she stayed with me and kept me warm and fed me on milk until I was big enough to look after myself.'

'That's what I'm doing,' said Otto. 'Waiting to be big enough to look after myself. When I am I can go to the sea, but at the moment I'm fed by the grown-up penguins who bring fish soup and squid soup and all sorts of nice things.'

'Oh, I get my own squid and fish now,' said the seal. 'I may meet you in the sea. Do penguins dive?'

'Yes. We have to to get our food,' said Otto.

'Well, I might pass you one day. My mother says that we are the best divers in the world. We can dive two thousand feet. How deep can you dive?'

'I don't know,' said Otto. 'But Claudius

did tell me that Weddell seals are very good divers and can dive deeper than us. What's your name? It seems silly to know somebody and not know his name. My name's Otto.'

'I haven't got a name,' said the seal. 'My mother always called me Pup and that was it.'

'Well, can I call you Pup?' asked Otto.

'Yes, Otto, you do that,' said Pup. 'Now I want to ask you something. Have you got any teeth?'

'Teeth?' said Otto. 'No, I don't think so. What are they?'

Pup opened his mouth and showed Otto his teeth. 'I need them,' he said. 'You see, when it's very cold I come up in the sea and find ice over my head. I have to get air to breathe, so I bite and bite the ice until I've made a breathing hole.'

'Oh, I've seen those,' said Otto. 'Just holes in the ice.'

'That's right,' said Pup. 'Well, that's what I have to have teeth for: because I have to breathe. It's hard work, though, if the ice is very thick.'

'Yes, your teeth do look as if you've been using them a lot,' said Otto. 'They're all sort of flat at the top. But then I don't know what they should look like anyway. So you've been to the sea. Is it fun?'

'Oh yes,' said Pup. 'I love it. And it's full of food. My mother taught me bit by bit how to catch shrimps and krill and squid, but now I can catch fish as well. She taught me everything I need to know. I do miss her.'

'I miss Claudius, too,' said Otto. 'He

taught me all I know, but he had to go to sea to feed before I had finished growing up. You were lucky to have your mother until you'd finished growing up. Anyway, I'd better stop talking and go down to the beach. Otherwise there won't be any food left for me. All the other chicks will have got it.'

'I'll come with you,' said Pup. 'It's time I got back to the sea, too. The sea's warmer than the ice.'

'Really?' said Otto.

'Yes,' said Pup.

So they went down the beach together, although Otto had to be very patient because Pup was so fat and slow. When they got there, Pup waved a flipper and disappeared into the sea, and Otto found an aunty to feed

him. On the way back to the rookery Otto
thought to himself, 'I wish I were a seal.
Penguins do take a long time to grow up.
But I suppose I'll get used to it.'

Growing

Otto was always hungry these days and the grown-ups always brought food from the sea. In fact, he began to enjoy meeting all the different grown-ups. Most of them were quite ordinary, but there were some specially nice ones. Justin was one of these. Otto had gone down towards the sea to look for someone to feed him and met Justin looking for someone to feed.

'My goodness,' Justin said, 'I'm hardly out of the sea. But all right, squid soup today.'

When Otto had finished he stood back and said, 'Delicious. I like squid soup.'

'Well, you'll be able to get your own soon. You're a big chap.'

'I'm first chick,' Otto said. 'Can you tell me something? The sea is getting nearer. Why?'

'The ice is breaking up at the edge of the sea because it's getting warmer. Antarctica's made of ice so it gets smaller every summer.'

'Oh, you sound just like Claudius,' Otto said. 'He always explained everything to me like that. I do miss him. He was my first father. He *was* good.'

'Of course he was good,' Justin said. 'I trained him. He was my chick once.'

'Claudius was *your* chick?' Otto said.

'You must be old!'

'Not that old,' said Justin. 'Anyway, let's go back to the rookery. We can talk on the way.'

Otto asked all the questions that he would have asked Claudius if he had still been around as they waddled back. At last Justin said:

'I think perhaps I *am* getting old. I'm tired. I can't answer any more questions.'

'Just one, Justin, please. Just one,' Otto said.

'All right, one,' said Justin.

'I just want to know when I can toboggan,' Otto said. 'I've seen the grown-ups slide across the ice very fast on their tummies. It does look fun.'

'You'll be able to toboggan when you

have your adult feathers,' Justin said.

'When will that be?'

'That's a second question,' Justin said. 'I said one.'

He saw Otto's head droop. He moved away but called back over his shoulder: 'Soon.'

Soon? Otto wanted to ask *how* soon, but he knew it was no good. He would just have to wait.

A few days later the cold wind began to blow and Otto knew he would have to get the smaller chicks into a warm huddle. He had an easy way of doing this now. All he had to do was find Gusto and send round a whisper that Gusto was going to tell stories. Then all the chicks would hurry over and press close to him to hear the stories, and there was the huddle. Gusto was chief storyteller now and he enjoyed his job. So Otto got Gusto to stand in a sheltered place and soon there was a big huddle of small penguins round him. Then bigger ones joined in round the edge.

One of these, a rather bad-tempered chick called Nap, began to make a fuss.

'What's Gusto doing in the centre of the huddle with the babies where it's warmest? He's as big as me. He should be on the outside,' he groused.

'He's doing a job,' Leo said.

'Yes, a very important job,' Otto joined in.

'He's big enough to be on the edge like me. Hey, Gusto,' Nap yelled.

'Shut up,' said Otto quietly.

'I won't shut up,' Nap said, giving Otto a push. 'Who do you think *you* are? Do you want a fight?'

'No,' said Otto, 'emperor penguins *don't* fight, because it's important for them to stay friends and huddle together to keep warm.'

'Coward,' said Nap. 'Come on, fight!'

'No,' Otto said. 'I'm an emperor penguin. Perhaps you're an adelie penguin. They squabble all the time. They lay their eggs in nests and even bicker over whose nest it is.

We're supposed to be sensible chaps.' Otto held his head in the air and looked at Nap down his beak. 'Go and find an adelie penguin to fight with or shut up.'

Nap shut up. There was sense in what Otto said.

Leo, who was on the other side of Otto, said, 'Where did you learn all that, Otto?'

'From Justin,' Otto said. 'I'm so glad I met him.'

He was, too, when Alex crept up to him after the huddle.

'Otto,' he said. 'I think I ought to tell you about something.'

'Well, go on then,' Otto said. 'What should you tell me about?'

'You're . . .' Alex swallowed, '. . . you're going bald!'

Otto looked down at himself. There were patches of down missing and thick white feathers showing through underneath.

'Yippee!' he shouted to the astonished Alex.

'Don't you mind?' Alex said.

'Mind?' said Otto. 'Going bald means I'm growing up.'

He rushed off to find Leo. Leo was second chick so he was probably shedding his down, too. He was. Soon all the older chicks had bald patches.

'We look an awful mess,' Leo said one morning. 'But it is exciting watching each other turn into proper penguins. You're getting a yellow collar, Otto, as well as black bits all down your back.'

'Am I?' Otto said. 'I wish I could see myself.'

Little Alex came up.

'I understand now,' he said to Otto. 'You are all going bald. I wish it would happen to me. I'm still fluffy all over.'

'It *will* happen to you, last chick. You'll just have to be very patient,' Otto said.

'I wish I were first chick, like you,' Alex said. 'You don't have to be patient like me.'

Otto laughed. 'Yes, I'm a very lucky chap.'

'Oh, you are silly, Alex,' Leo said. 'It

takes just as long to grow up whether you hatch early or late.'

'Yes, but it must seem longer when you're the last one,' said Otto. 'Poor Alex. Never mind. At least you'll know what's coming next all the time. We haven't a clue. But I suppose we'll get used to it.'

Knowing

But this time Otto and Leo could not get
used to it. They had to know what was going
to happen next.

'We'll ask a grown-up,' said Otto. 'Come
on, it's feeding time anyway.'

So they set off towards the sea to meet
the adults coming up with food for them. Otto
found an aunt, Cathy; Leo found an uncle,
Julius. When they met again at the rookery

Otto and Leo rushed towards each other.

'What have you found out?' Otto asked.

'We'll be able to go to sea ourselves soon,' Leo said.

'When?' asked Otto.

'Julius was a fat lot of help. He just said we'd *know* when.'

'Cathy said the same,' Otto said. 'She said that when we're ready a group of us will go together. The sea is full of life and we just have to swim around and collect it for ourselves.'

'Swim?' asked Leo. 'What's that?'

'It's like flying, but in the water. We waggle our flippers. Claudius told me about it. It's what penguins are best at, swimming. I'm longing to try, but we have to wait until we've lost all our down.'

'Why?' said Leo. 'You should know. You seem to know everything.'

'Because I say so,' Otto said firmly. He had no idea. Perhaps down soaked up the water and got in the way. He'd have to find a grown-up who knew next feeding time.

The trouble was, not all adults were good at answering questions, or would try. In the end it was another chick who told him. A lady, first chick of another huddle. He met her on the edge of the rookery. She greeted him with: 'You've shed all your down. You're ready.'

Otto gaped at her. 'All of it? Really?'

She waddled all round him. 'Yes. You've got all your adult feathers. Dense oily feathers which will make you waterproof. What about me?'

Otto waddled round her.

'You've one tiny tuft of down left on your back. Shall I peck it off for you?'

'No. Thank you, though it was kind of you to offer. But it has to come off by itself when it's ready – when the feathers underneath are oily enough.'

'I see,' Otto said. 'What's your name?'

'Josie.'

'Oh, thank you, Josie. You must have had a good father to tell you things.'

'Yes, I did. But most of my huddle think I'm a bossy know-all.'

'Me too,' Otto said. 'It *is* nice to meet someone like you.'

So they enjoyed a good grumble about the problems of being first chick in their huddles. At last they thought they had better go back, so they parted.

'See you tomorrow, Josie, perhaps,' Otto said. 'Goodbye for now.'

'Goodbye, Otto. I've learned a lot from you.'

Otto had learned a lot too. When he bumped into Leo, Leo cried, 'You're a proper penguin, Otto – all black and white and yellow. Am I?'

Otto waddled round him.

'You only have two bits of down left and they're on your back.'

'Oh, Otto, peck 'em off,' Leo begged.

'Please, Otto.'

'No,' Otto said. 'I wouldn't be doing you a good turn at all. The feathers underneath can't be ready yet.'

'Oh, all right, Mr Know-all. I'll get someone else to peck them off.'

'No, Leo, please wait. The thing is, your feathers have to get properly oily before you go in the sea. You might sink otherwise.'

'Sink? You told me that penguins are marvellous swimmers.'

'We are. When our feathers are ready. You won't have long to wait now.'

'*Wait*,' groaned Leo. 'We're always waiting for something.'

'Yes, we are. I'm having to wait for you before we go to sea. I'm not going without you.'

'Oh, Otto, you're going on waiting just
for me?'

'Yes,' grinned Otto. 'I'll get used to it.'

All at sea

Otto could not get a meal next day. 'You're not a chick. You're a penguin,' the adults kept saying.

'Only just,' he cried. But nobody would feed him.

So that's what they'd meant when they'd said he would know when he was ready. They wouldn't *feed* him when he was ready, so hunger would drive him to the sea.

Soon there was quite a crowd of angry young penguins standing at the edge of the rookery complaining about the mean adults, and Leo was among them. He came waddling towards Otto.

'What do we do now?' he wailed. 'We're starving.'

'What do you think we do? Where shall we find squid and fish and krill and all the other things that grown-ups keep bringing us?'

'The sea!' Leo said. 'Come on, everybody. To sea!'

He started to waddle in the right direction but Otto shot past him on his tummy.

'Come on,' Otto cried. 'Toboggan. It's much quicker.'

Soon they were all tobogganing, shooting across the ice on their fat feathery fronts, propelled by their strong flippers. Their steering wasn't very good at first and there were a lot of collisions. Otto met Josie again by bumping into her.

'*Whoops* – sorry!' he said. 'Oh, Josie!'

'Yes, it's me,' said Josie. 'Isn't this fun? I've always wanted to do this.'

'Me too,' Otto said. 'The only thing is, is it all right for us to leave our huddles to look after themselves now? I feel a bit guilty.'

'Don't worry,' said Josie, pushing herself along beside him. 'It's warm enough now. They'll be all right. They'll join us soon. Forget them. Come on. Let's have a race. I'll beat you to the sea.'

She shot off in front of him and Otto was so busy chasing her that he forgot all about his chicks.

But his job wasn't quite over. When they reached the edge of the sea all the young penguins bunched together, afraid to go on. It was up to Otto and Josie and the other first

chicks to go in first. There were six of them.
They looked at each other. Otto was scared,
but he remembered what Claudius had said:
'Penguins look after each other.'

'Come on!' he yelled. 'Food!' and
splashed in. He leaned forward and moved
his flippers. Yes, he could swim. In fact,
swimming was even faster than tobogganing.
Soon he was swimming about on top of the
water and calling out to Leo.

'Come on, it's easy.'

Leo and all the others were soon in, but
after the joy of finding that they could swim
they began to remember something.

'Well, where's the food?' one of them
shouted.

'Underneath you,' replied Josie. 'We have
to dive for it, like this.'

She disappeared head first. The others copied her. Otto decided that this was the best bit yet, swimming under water. It was so interesting down there.

He wasn't hungry very much longer. He met a fish, opened his beak and swallowed it. He went to the bottom and saw something moving under a rock. He grabbed its leg and pulled. Well, now he knew what a squid looked like. That went the same way as the fish.

After a few krill, he torpedoed back up to the surface. It was quite a long way up. He was just going to start swimming back to the beach when he saw Josie. She was looking up at a cliff of ice. Suddenly she dived into the water and disappeared. Perhaps she was still hungry.

But then she came up again – and *up* was the word. She leaped clean out of the water and right up the cliff.

'Be careful,' Otto shouted.

But he needn't have bothered. Josie looked down at him from the top of the cliff where she had landed and shouted, 'You can do it, Otto. My father told me about this. It's penguins' leap. You're a penguin, aren't you?'

Otto needed no more urging than that. He tried to leap, but fell back with a splash.

Josie laughed down at him. 'That's not the way!' she shouted. 'Dive a long way down and then torpedo up as fast as you can and just keep going.'

Otto did what he was told.

He found himself on top of the ice cliff near to Josie. He had landed on his feet as if he had been doing it all his life. Oh, he did feel pleased with himself. He could toboggan, he could swim, he could feed himself and now he could leap.

Josie came towards him. 'Well, Otto, do you like being a penguin?'

'I'll get used to it,' he said happily.

This is Suzy.

Suzy is a small stripy cat.

Suzy likes: living in France,
chasing butterflies and being
stroked the wrong way.

Suzy doesn't like: getting lost . . .

Read another Jill Tomlinson
and find out more.

This is Pat.

Pat is a little sea otter.

She loves asking questions.

But what happens when
no one knows the answers?

Clever Pat just has to find
things out for herself!

Read another Jill Tomlinson
and find out more.

This is Hilda.

Hilda is a small, speckled hen.

Hilda likes cornflakes, fire-engines and visiting her auntie.

But there is one thing that Hilda would like more than anything else . . .

Read another Jill Tomlinson and find out more.

This is Pongo.

Pongo is a little gorilla.

He lives in the mountains in Africa.

Pongo wants to be as brave
and clever as his dad.

He wants a big silver chest to thump!

But first he has to grow up.

Read another Jill Tomlinson
and find out more.

EGMONT PRESS: ETHICAL PUBLISHING

Egmont Press is about turning writers into successful authors and children into passionate readers – producing books that enrich and entertain. As a responsible children's publisher, we go even further, considering the world in which our consumers are growing up.

Safety First
Naturally, all of our books meet legal safety requirements. But we go further than this; every book with play value is tested to the highest standards – if it fails, it's back to the drawing-board.

Made Fairly
We are working to ensure that the workers involved in our supply chain – the people that make our books – are treated with fairness and respect.

Responsible Forestry
We are committed to ensuring all our papers come from environmentally and socially responsible forest sources.

**For more information, please visit our website at
www.egmont.co.uk/ethical**

MIX
Paper
FSC   FSC® C018306

Egmont is passionate about helping to preserve the world's remaining ancient forests. We only use paper from legal and sustainable forest sources, so we know where every single tree comes from that goes into every paper that makes up every book.

This book is made from paper certified by the Forestry Stewardship Council (FSC®), an organisation dedicated to promoting responsible management of forest resources. For more information on the FSC, please visit **www.fsc.org**. To learn more about Egmont's sustainable paper policy, please visit **www.egmont.co.uk/ethical**.